this
little ORCHARD
book belongs to

....

....

ORCHARD BOOKS
96 Leonard Street, London EC2A 4XD
Orchard Books Australia
14 Mars Road, Lane Cove, NSW 2066
1 86039 985 1 (hardback)
1 86039 987 8 (paperback)
First published in Great Britain in 1999

A CIP catalogue record for this book is available from the British Library.
Printed in Italy

Freddie has a haircut

Nicola Smee

little ORCHARD

"It's time for a haircut, Freddie!" says Mum.

It certainly is!

Bear wants to come and watch.

"Hello Freddie! Hello Bear!" says Bob, the hairdresser.

Bob is making
my hair wet
so that it's
easier to cut.

I tell him to be careful not to snip my ears!

Snip
Snip

goo

All done!
Not bad!

"Here, pick a lollipop Freddie, and take one home for Bear," says Bob.

Thank you Bob !

Bob's Hair Salon
Dad, can I have mine cut like Freddie's?

Freddie you look LOVELY!